T0082724

SUPREME

SUPREME

JOHNQUES LUPOE

SUPREME

iUniverse books may be ordered through booksellers or by contacting:

iUniverse
1663 Liberty Drive
Bloomington, IN 47403
www.iuniverse.com
844-349-9409

Because of the dynamic nature of the Internet, any web addresses or links contained in this book may have changed since publication and may no longer be valid. The views expressed in this work are solely those of the author and do not necessarily reflect the views of the publisher, and the publisher hereby disclaims any responsibility for them.

Any people depicted in stock imagery provided by Getty Images are models, and such images are being used for illustrative purposes only. Certain stock imagery © Getty Images.

ISBN: 978-1-6632-2063-9 (sc)
ISBN: 978-1-6632-2064-6 (e)

Library of Congress Control Number: 2021907672

Print information available on the last page.

iUniverse rev. date: 04/12/2021

1

June 11,2019 "Now Juan you know your brother is going to be very happy to see you, so don't make him look like a fool" Ms.Virginia stated as she pulled inside of the parking lot. Noticing that they had boosted up the security from the last time he had come to visit his brother. As they walked inside of the building he spotted Pharaoh standing there in his all white cloak,looking like a real doctor.

Beginning to smile from ear to ear as his brother began to notice who he was. Making their way over to each other, they extended their arms to embrace each other with a hug. "Look at you man you are all grown up now" "Yea prison will do that to you especially if you done the time I have"

"Yeah 13 years is a long time and I'm sorry for not coming to visit you like I used to. Things have been real busy around here lately"

"So what is it that you do around here at D.N.A and what does that mean?"

"Well it's exactly what it says. We just decode your D.N.A to make it better"

"Nigga how in the hell you gone make somebody D.N.A better?"

"Well I will explain all of that to you as I give you and moma the grand tour"

As they walked around the company and got a better insight on what it is that Pharaoh did. Juan thought to himself that all of this was just another way for the government to keep track of people.

All of the bullshit like 23 &me, ancestry.com, when they help you track down your bloodline the government has your D.N.A on file from there on. So if you ever do anything wrong they can lock you up because they already have your D.N.A on file.

"Little bruh do you follow me?"

"Yeah nigga I'm listening,I was just thinking about something"

"Oh yea like what we are always open for new ideals"

"Nah bruh this wasn't no idea here,this was an assumption"

"Oh lawd there you go,I see you still the same." "Man I aint even said nothing" Juan laughed "Yeah bruh but I know you that's the whole thing. Here do me a favor,take this card and go place it inside of that slot. But make sure you put it in right side up"

"Ok I got you, why you making a big deal out of this little funky card"

"Juan this just ain't no card, you have to be careful with it"

"Yeah yeah I got you,I ain't slow"

Juan walked off to place the card inside of the slot. Standing there waiting for the slot to open,he glanced back at Pharaoh. Smiling and nodding his head trying to get Pharaoh to introduce him to the little red nurse that he was talking to. Dropping the card inside of the slot while still eyeing the sexy little nurse. It dawned on him to check the card and make sure it was inserted the right way. But before he could take the card back out the tray retracted.

A red light lit up, and before Pharaoh could tell Juan to move it was too late. It was like a small atomic bomb was set off. The radioactive elements came bursting out of the glass walled chamber. Hitting his skin as the force blew him out of the building and deep into the woods. Hitting another tree before plummeting to the ground. Kneeling down on all fours as the elements became one with his blood. Seeing the elements moving through his veins he dug his fingers into the ground.

Closing his eyes to an eclipse,seeing the virus taking over his body and blood cells. Panicking from not knowing if he was about to die or what. Juan hopped up and took off running. Trying to make it back to his mom and brother before anything else happened to him. Looking at the damage he caused to the forest as he ran back through it. He started to wonder how he was even still alive. Everything was going by in slow motion, but it felt like his legs were going a million miles an hour.

Realizing that he was moving in supersonic speed and that's why everything else was in slow motion. Coming out of the woods,to see the big whole in the wall from where he came out of. He took back off running and leaped in the air. Landing back inside of the building, Juan yelled for his mother and brother before he collapsed.

FLASHBACK

"Supreme!!!.... Juan Johnson if you don't bring yo ass in this house right this instant!!!!"

Smacking his teeth as he dropped his head and headed to the house. Feeling embarrassed with his moma standing outside in her bathrobe and house shoes. And to top it off she had her hair rollers in and a green facemask on. As he walked past her he questioned her why he had to come inside. "Boy you don't pay no damn bills here, so get yo ass in the house"

"But mom everybody still hanging out"

"Boy it's 9pm at night you ain't got no business outside this late"

"But I'm right there,it ain't like you cant see me" "Child I'm not about to go back and forth with you"

3

Growing up his face as he stumped away. Virginia slapped him across the back of his head. Juan embraced for the hit,then took off running up the stairs."Why your little brother can't be more like you?" Virginia asked Pharaoh as she shook her head out of pity. Inhaling and exhaling deeply before leaving back out of the living room. Knowing that Juan was just like his father,always wanted to hang in the streets.

Before she could clean the melon scented face mask off of her face Pharaoh was calling her. Racing back downstairs to see Juan standing there kooin handcuffs. She broke down in tears before she could even ask the officers what happened or if they were taking him in.

"What did he get handcuffed for?"

"Well he was down the street jumping on two guys twice his size"

"Boy get yo ass in this damn house, I thought I was about to lose you"

"Well ma'am we could have but we thought bring him back to you was better"

"Thank you for not taking him in and I'll handle it from here"

As she walked in the house she pushed the door shut. Looking at him with a look that would kill while she grabbed him by his shirt and shook him.

"Juan Supreme Johnson what is wrong with you? Don't I tell and show you that I love you enough to keep you out of the streets?"

"Yea ma that's why I got to fighting in the first place"

"Boy you are just like your damn father,so damn hot headed"

"Darius and Calvin was talking about how fine you where and

what they wanted to do to you" Them lol boys just messing with you, you know gooden damn well I don't want your little friends"

Laughing at him before telling him to go to his room and stay there for the rest of the night. Ask you one took off upstairs Virginia yelled out "make sure you take your bath while you're up there". Meanwhile Pharaoh was just completing his science project. Using a pickle to light up a light bulb. It made him feel like a mad scientist. Standing there smiling from ear to ear. Virginia gave him a high five and told him congratulations. He quickly cleaned up his mess so he could go check on his little brother. "Yo Supreme where you at?"

Slowly waking from the sound of Pharaoh's voice, Juan thought he was still dreaming. Barely opening his eyes he noticed that he was laying in a hospital bed hooked up to all kinds of machines. As he lifted his head up to look around the room. Pharaoh told him to take it easy because he needed the rest.

Laying back down before asking where was his moma.

"She's outside lil bro, I'll bring her in once you have rested"

"Bruh just incase I don't make it I love y'all" "It's no need to worry lil bro your going to be fine"

Before he could say anything back he was out like a light. Everyone paused for a second to see what his next reaction would be, then turned to the machines. Amazed from how his blood reacted to the chemical compound elements. They begin to draw blood and run lab tests. With every experiment they had done, trying thus far was never a success this fast. It always took a few tries and test runs.

2

Two days later Juan was released from D.N.A. with no signs of a change they thought it was another failure. His blood was just reacting in a way they never seen before. They told the agent to keep tabs on his every move just in case something changed. But what they didn't know Juan wasn't just any average guy. Doing time in the GDOC made him pay attention to his surroundings even more than before.

And it was easy for him to spot the guy that had been trailing him since you left Decoding Nucleic Acids Agency. Looking for a quick duck off spot so he could get away from the little spy. He quickly went inside of a restaurant and came back out on the patio. Happen over the small real than an inch and out just enough to look around the corner. Watching the agent enter inside of the building he noticed that his hand matched the wall.

He quickly snatches his hand off the wall. But that wasn't the only problem; his whole body had taken the shape and color of the wall. Juan panicked and took off running. Everything was happening to him all over again. The more he Panic the more things started to happen to him his chemical balance was off track.

The only thing he could think of was to get somewhere safe and hide. Luckily he didn't have to go far; his apartment in Atlantic Station was just around the corner. As he made it to his apartment he grabbed the doorknob and his hand became one with the knob. Quickly pushing the door open it came off the hinges. Standing there holding the door in his hand he heard a door opening. He quickly stepped inside and laid the door over the doorway. Pasting back and forth trying to decide whether he was going to call his brother or handle his business on his own.

"Nah i'll just chill for now" he thought to himself.

Making his way around the apartment changing into different objects and textures are things. Trying to find out what he can and can't do. Knowing that he had a camo and shape-shifting ability was the only beginning. All kinds of thoughts went through his head. Being able to get away with so much dirt he thought about how much he could help out his family.

Being super fast and strong was just a plus. Hours of playing around with his ability. It was time to take it to the streets. Coming down the flight of stairs he spotted the agent coming through the door." Time to have a little fun"

Juan spoke to himself as he shot pass the agent. Picking his pocket as he shot by him.

Feeling a gust of wind 30 seconds after Juan had been left out of the building. The agent shook from the slight chill. Looking around trying to see what the breeze came from. He headed upstairs and radio back to the office. Letting them know that he was back at the test subject house. As he got off the elevator and walked closer to the apartment,

he noticed that the door wasn't on the hinges.

He quickly called for backup as he entered the apartment. Cautiously walking around to find anything out of the ordinary. Everything was intact just like it was, when the company gave it to him.

Meanwhile Juan I was at a local bar enjoying himself. As the time passed by people came and left. Juan moved from out of the back corner up to the bar. Feeling good and a little tipsy he began to flirt with the bartender. She looked like a Scarlett Johansson stunt double. With long red hair and pretty blue eyes.

The more the liquor took over his body the smoother he got with his words. Seeing that she was going for his smooth talking he asked for the number. After receiving the number, he winked his eyes at her while giving her a tip.

guys talking about the young lady that was a few steps in front of him.

"Now that's what you call a lady,look at all that ass"

"Hell yeah I would love to be her bath water" That brought an idea to mind. Following behind her as she left out of the bar. He couldn't tell if it was the liquor or what, but it seemed to him every chick he saw looked like a celebrity. This sexy redbone put him in the mind of Cardi B. And that made him want to follow through with his crazy little idea. Doing all of that time behind the walls looking magazines of half naked chicks made him have nothing but lust in his eyes.

As she entered the building of her condo, Juan quietly slid in behind her.

Taking shape of the things around him so he could go unseen. As he took the shape of the blue couch, he noticed that his clothes didn't change with him. It looked like someone had just laid some clothes across the couch. Luckily the security guard wasn't at his post. Quickly removing himself off the couch to behind the couch.

off on. Then took off up the stairs. Coming out of his clothes so he could go unseen as he followed her out the elevator and into her apartment. Headed straight to the bathroom and started her bathwater. Juan followed right behind her. As she left back out of the bathroom Juan slid right inside of the tub. Changing right into a water form.

Walking back into the bathroom in a cream colored robe. She checked the water before shutting it off. Then lit her candles, before she came out of her robe and climbed the side of the tub. Grabbing her wash rag out of the water and squeezed it. Letting the water hit the top of her chest and run down.

Each bead of water that rolled down her body you can see a small face in it. Juan was loving his new gift. Being able to do things that most folks dreamed about. He shelf back and forth from being the water one minute and the rag the next. It was like all of his perverted little fantasies coming to life.

As she dropped the rag into the water, he changed back into the water. You could see his face in the soap bubbles as he washed her laying there with her eyes closed. Do you want to talk to himself that she could be a keeper, he just had to find a way to meet her. But before his thoughts went any farther, she broke wind. Juan's face disappeared from the surface of the water. He began swirling around in the tub.

Tossing the chick all around, making her swirl up and out of the tub. She wasted no time running out of the bathroom.

Meanwhile Juwan had knocked over the tub stopper and went down the drain. Taking the sewage system to the nearest Ally to his apartment. Pushing the sewer top off and slowly peeking out of it. As he came out of the manhole looked for something to cover him up. Grabbing to metal trash can lids and took off into his building.

Having no time to wait on the elevator he took the flight of stairs. As you came speeding through the stairwell door he bumped into one of his neighbors. Dropping both can lids on the ground. Fumbling trying to pick up the lids,

while keeping the small dog off of him. Once he stood up he locked eyes with his neighbor.

She looked like she was black and Asian. She had a pretty brown skin tone with long silky black hair. A gorgeous face and a banging body. She couldn't have been no more than 5'5 or 5'6. Her eyes were mesmerizing with the pretty little slant that they had to them.

"Nice to meet you, I'm Juan" he said as he reached out his hand to greet her, while dropping the lid.

"Umm you might want to cover all of that up but I'm Precious"

"Oh that you are!"

"look like you're having a little bit of a rough night"

"I was until now how about you let me take you out for a drink?"

"I probably would have took you up on that offer, but me and you like this and all of the crazy stuff that went on earlier today I'm going to have to pass"

"hold up what crazy stuff?"

"they had the whole building surrounded with a bunch of guys dressed in all black with all kind of tactical gear"

Standing there with a deranged look on his face before he took off running. All she could see was his back side as he ran down the hallway.

"But wait I didn't get your number" she giggled as she watched him run away. Thinking to herself " now that brother was fine" as her and the pooch walked off.

Arriving back at his apartment he noticed that the door was fixed. Turning the knob and gently pushing it open. Looking around before actually walking inside. As he walked in and closed the door a funny feeling came over him that it felt like someone was watching him but there weren't any signs on where it was coming from.

He jumped in the shower to clean off. And as soon as he sat on the edge of the bed a phone rang. He looked behind him and a starling motion looking for the phone. To see it sitting on the nightstand by the window. Picking up the phone to answer it.

"who is this and how did you put my phone back in here?"

"Well Mr. Johnson our agency is full of surprises"

"okay but you still not telling me anything"

"how about we talk it over breakfast tomorrow at IHOP"

"Man... see a lot of crazy shit be happening when people like you want to meet up with people like me at restaurants"

"what do you mean Mr. Johnson I'm just trying to have breakfast"

"you ain't never seen Triple X, The Avengers or any other hero movie"

"maybe but I'll text you which one"

Before Juan could get out another word the phone hung up and a text was coming in. He didn't even bother to open it, he just laid back on the bed and closed his eyes.

3

10am the next morning Juan was awakened by the sound of his phone going off.

"Hello"

"Your late Mr.Johnson"

"Yeah nigga I know,wasn't planning on meeting you there anyways"

"glad to be informed of that news, we have already made plans for something like this"

The phone hung up and you won't roll back over. Within the matter of seconds, his window shattered. He jumped off the bed and took off running down his hallway. To be met by the tactical squad a Precious was telling him about. Feeling chapped he placed his hands on his head. And waiting for the first person to make their move.

As soon as one got reached in to restrain him he took off. Grabbing the guy by his hand and twisting it. Pushing him into the crowd then releases him. Turning around with a roundhouse kick, kicking a guy in the chest from the other side. The more he fought the more they closed in on him. For a quick second everything began to move in slow motion. Juan had closed his eyes and when they reopened he was stronger than ever.

With each blow an agent went flying. Running through the crowd taking them out two at a time. Realizing that they couldn't stop him they started shooting. East Penn closet. They shot atl him repealed off his body. The more agency took out the more kept coming. He knew that he had to out think them.

Moving in supersonic speed everything around him slows down. He undressed one of the agents and went out the door and his uniform. As he got to the entrance of the building he slowed down and walked right out. Passing by other gods as if he was one of them. Making it far enough to not be noticed before he broke into a car and drove off. 20 minutes later he arrived at his mother's house.

Entering inside the house he yelled out for his mom.

"Say ma where you at?"

"I'm back here in the back Juan!"

Walking through the house took him back down memory lane. All of the chicks that he had sneaking in and out of the house. And not to mention all of the trouble he got into. Walking into the back room to see his mama kickback watching TV. About a smile to his face. Knowing that his moma hasn't changed one bit.

"Come on in here and tell me what you need help with now"

"nothing I just came by to check on you"Juan chuckled

"yeah you still lying I see, you know your brother done called me"

"man Pharaoh some bullshit he always talking too much"

"he just trying to look out for his little brother, you know he is crazy about you"

"yeah I know but dang"

"He want me to tell you to turn yourself back into the agency in so they can run more tests on you"

"Ma you know that ain't going to happen, that's just I turning myself into a jail"

"oh yeah I know how you are but besides that how you feeling"

"feeling great, like a new man"

13

"well that's good, I hope you're hungry" Following his mom to the kitchen, the aroma of a home-cooked meal hit his nose. He squeezed by her and went to open up pots to look inside. Virginia popped him upside the head and told him to wash his hands before he started messing around with the food.

"Boy you still the same"

"What?! Ma you know how long it's been since I had a good meal"

"Boy go sit your nappy head ass down and that's dinner anyways"

"So what we bout to eat?"

Smacking her teeth before telling him that she has some leftover chicken she was about to warm up. It ain't even been 10 minutes since you got here and you already working my nerves, Virginia implied. Then began to think to herself, on how much you really miss Juan around the house. As she placed the chicken in the microwave, the house phone rang. Picking the phone up off the counter to answer it.

"Hello"

"Hey have you heard from you Juan yet?"

"yeah baby he's right here... well he was just at the table"

"He must have known it was me. Well look if he comes back I need you to tell him this for me"

"okay what is it?"

"tell him that I'm sorry and I made a big mistake but I really need him to come down to the agency"

"well you know your brother ain't going to turn himself in"

"Well ma, if he loves us he will"

"wait what are you trying to say?"

"just tell him big bro need his help like the old days"

"Hello!!Hello!! Pharaoh are you there?"

As the phone hung up in her ear, Juan was sitting back at the table like he never left. Virginia hung up the phone and sat it down, then turned around to see Juan sitting back at the table.

"Where did you go so fast?"

"What you mean I just went into the living room"

"Well that was your brother and he told me to tell you that he needs your help and for you to come back to the center"

"Yeah right that's just a trick, Ma you know I ain't going for that"

"I don't know Juan you might want to check it out"

"Man ma where that food at I ain't got time to play with Pharaoh"

She just looked at him and shook her head. She knew that it was going to be hard to get him back to the agency. Virginia placed the plate of chicken on the table right along with a big bottle of Texas Pete hot sauce. Juan opened the bag of Hawiian rolls and dug in. Fucking up the chicken like it was his first day out all over again.

After he was done eating, he took a seat on the sofa and turned on the t.v. Flipping through the channels trying to find something to watch. He found an old X-Men movie. "Oh hell nah! I use to like this shit, look at my dumb ass now. I done turned into one of these motherfukers for real" Juan chuckled to himself as he changed the channel. As he searched channels he realized that it really wasn't nothing on so he turned back to X-Men.

Slowly drifting off to sleep, Juan begins dreaming. Dreaming that he was standing in front of the agency. And out of nowhere Wolverine appeared up telling him "Lets go". They both took off running inside of the building. To be met by an army of experiments that was turned in to agents. Wasting no time Juan started fighting.

He was wiping out the agents with no problem,but they just kept multiplying.

The harder he fought the more they piled up on him. He was engulfed by experiments and the only thing he could hear was Pharaoh telling him to dig deep. Generating power out of nowhere,you could see a bright light shining through the pile. And within seconds they went flying everywhere,as the energy bomb went off. He stood in the middle of the floor glowing.

Awaken from the sound of gun shots. Juan rolled off the couch and started looking around. Realizing that it was the t.v, he got off the floor and sat back on the couch. Trying to fully awake before he started moving. He heard his moma in the kitchen moving around. Making his way to the kitchen, he just stood in the doorway looking at his moma. As she took the roast out of the oven and sat it on the stove.

She pulled off a little piece of the roast beef to taste, Juan cleared his throat.

"oh boy you scared me"

"yeah cuz he eaten that out the pot" Juan spoke in the laughter voice

"Boy is my house, now go get freshen up for dinner"

"yes ma'am masa is there anything else"

"boy you better gone get out of here with that foolishness"

Juan went to the restroom to freshen up. Running water over his hands then splashing it on his face. As he cold his eyes to wipe the water off his face, Pharaoh appeared in the darkness. Quickly open his eyes to begin staring in the mirror at himself. Taking a deep breath before hitting the counter.

"Dammit Pharaoh" Juan frustrated Lee yelled as he rolled his head walking out of the bathroom.

Taking the seat at the table, Virginia noticed that something was on his mind. She looked at him as she set his plate down in front of him. "What's wrong Juan?"

"What do you mean what's wrong? Ma look at me everything is wrong"

"Baby you are looking at this all wrong. God don't make mistakes"

"Ma all I wanted to do was come home and get to the money, so I can help you out around here. I wanted to take care of you for a change"

"Juan, you have been different your whole life. Why do you think I name you Supreme and your brother Pharaoh? Y'all are Kings black gods why do you think they fear our race like they do. Baby use this gift for a good thing and that's how you will be helping me. And just remember what I always tell you to be the best you can be in whatever it is you do."

Juan sat they're listening to his mother as she gave him the game. Knowing that it wasn't going to be easy, trying to be the best at a game he never knew nothing about. And the only way to be the best is to learn from the best. As he finished eating he slid his plate up and told his mother to call his brother. And inform him that he would be there first thing smokin in the morning.

Virginia smiled at the fact that she knew, her son was about to set a tone for whatever it was to come. She picked up the phone and called Pharaoh just as Juan wanted her to.

4

The next morning Juan arrived at the company, he was escorted inside like a fugitive. Standing in the middle of the lobby made him think about his dream. As he stood there a white man in a very expensive suit came walking down the hall. He was accompanied by Pharaoh and another doctor. But the other gave off a bad vibe. He had two other guys with him.

"welcome home Mr. Johnson"

"yeah whatever bruh this ain't my home"

"Well it kinda is because this is where you was made"

"my mama made me and if it wasn't for my brother I wouldn't be here"

"yeah that's why we're so proud of Dr Johnson.Umm I think we need to call one of you by your first name so we won't get things mixed up around here."

"do what you want because I ain't going to be here that long"

"Whoa whoa whoa slow down there, this is not going to be a one day process"

"Yo Pharaoh you need to come holla at me before I get active around this bitch"

Pharaoh looked at Juan and placed his finger over his mouth, signalling for him to be quiet. Juan frowned up his face as he watched Pharaoh humble himself down to talk to the man.

"Aye my man what's your name again?" "Oh so now you want to talk to me?"

"Man I just want to know who I will be working for"

"Oh why you just didn't say so, I am Mr.Bush

Beans"

"Hold up yo name Bush Beans like the food?" "Yes but there is no relation"

"man I know you got picked on your childhood, and that's probably why you want to take over the world uh?"

"I like you already, good sense of humor. Dr. Johnson show him his living quarters"

Pharaoh escorted Juan to his room then slid him a note. While closing the door, Pharaoh told him to change clothes and to be ready in five minutes. As the door shut Juan turned and looked around at the room.

It put him in the mind of being locked up all over again. But the only difference was the room,it was an upgrade. Grabbing the uniform then examining it before laying it across the bed.

Checking to see if it was a tracking device or something that could control his body if he didnt listen. Then he decided to open the letter that Pharaoh gave him. He quickly read it and then balled it up. The letter read as followed:

Lil bruh I need you to follow my lead around here. I'm on to something but I can't do it without you. Every since they have tested your blood things have been getting out of hand. So please keep your cool and until I tell you other words.

As soon as he finished reading it his door popped back open. Juan snatched his shirt off and stood there. Waiting to see who was about to come in.

"Time is up"

"Man if you don't get yo Marvin the Martian looking ass out of here I'm getting dressed" "If the boss didn't need you I would come in there and whip yo ass, now hurry up!"

"Whatever lil nigga I'd like to see that now give me 2 minutes"

The guard left back out the room and stood at the door. Juan finished getting dressed,then threw the note in the toilet. Before leaving out the room he took a deep breath and turned his game face on. Following behind the guard as they made their way through the hallway. Juan heard screaming coming from behind different doors.

Not really sure what all the screaming was about or who it was, raised a red flag for him. Arriving at the drop off point the guard turned to Juan and mumbled let's see how tough you are now, then walked off. Juan smirked at him before walking inside the room. As he entered the room he saw Pharaoh standing at the end of the hallway waiting on him. As soon as he walked up Pharaoh jumped straight into what they were about to do. Not giving Juan time to say a word.

"Juan this is our training area for hand to hand combat"

"Hold up I thought this agency was to help people better their D.N.A not for making soldiers"

Pharaoh grabbed Juan by the arm and pushed him up against the wall.

"Look bro I told you to just follow my led here I can't talk how I want to right now"

"Well you need to find sometime because I don't like feeling left out"

"OK well this time you just got to trust in your brother"

"Alight you can back up off me now"

Pharaoh walked off and went down the flight of stairs. Slowly following behind his brother as he kept his eyes on the competition.

Just by the looks of everyone, Juan felt as if he could take them. But he didn't want to count his chickens before they hatched. He knew that they all were there for a reason. As soon as his feet hit the padded floor Pharaoh attacked him.

Fighting just good enough to keep Pharaoh off of him. The whole attack caught him off guard. Going back and forth with Pharaoh, Juan knew that this could be the best time for them to talk. As soon as Pharaoh made his next move Juan rushed in on him. Taking him down to the floor, then whispered in his ear "Now's your time". Pharaoh paused for a brief second and looked at him with a puzzled look. Juan tightened up on his grip and looked at him with a stupid smirk.

Pharaoh caught on to what he was saying and doing, then went back to tussling.

"You are smarter than you look lil bro"

"Tell me something that I don't know like what's going on around here"

"Oh yea as you can see they are creating a team of super human"

"Why and is the whole thing about bettering your DNA just a cover up?

"No not at all we really help people but in the process we discover a chemical genetic that makes you have super powers"

"Ok but that's still not telling me why"

Before Pharaoh could open his mouth they rang a bell indicating that it was time to switch opponents. Juan stood there waiting for his opponent, until he felt a tug on his pants leg. Looking down trying to see where the tugging came from. Within seconds Juan was knocked to the ground, with a female towering over him. "Where the hell you come from"

"Element of surprise baby, so are you gonna lay around or are we gone fight?"

Sweeping her feet from under her then climbed on top. Penning her to the mat then gave her a quick smile. That only made her more frustrated. Using a hip thrusting motion to buck out of the pen. They both rolled to opposite sides and jumped up. Standing there in their fighting stands waiting for one another to make a move.

They begin to admire each other. Juan looked at her from head to toe. Watching how the spandex hugged her curves. Her pretty skin tone and beautiful eyes set off a little twinkle in his eye. Something was going through her head as they stood there. She shook out of it and told one of the fighters next to them to switch with her.

"Hold up where you going" "You not ready for combat"

"What do you mean I'm not ready?" "You got other things on your mind" "So you are a mind reader now" "Maybe"

Taking his focus off of her after from getting hit in the mouth. Juan knew that he couldn't let her be the reason why he got his ass handed to him. Each person that stood in front of him he gave them his all. Every so often he would glance over and catch her watching him. After so many hours had done pass, they finally rung the alarm.

Everyone grabbed their things and headed back to their living area. Juan tried his best to catch up with old girl, but each time he got close someone would interfere. Getting pulled over by Pharaoh when he was only a few steps away made him frustrated.

"Man bruh what's up I'm trying to do something"

"I know that's why I stopped you"

"What was I trying to do since you know everything?"

"Come on you ain't gone be able to do nothing with her"

"Damn was it that obvious"

"A little but look you did good out there today, I didn't know you was that good"

"Yea I did a little training while I was down with this guy named Black Jesus"

"Well tomorrow will be a little different so get some rest"

"Aye when we gone finish talking"

Pharaoh put his finger over his mouth and winked his eye as the door closed. Juan stood there in the window looking at his brother, he could tell that he wasn't really himself at times.

5

"Trays up sleeping beauty" Juan heard as the flap on the door came down. He looked back at the door then covered his head. Taking a few minutes to get up. This whole scene made him feel as if he was back locked down. As he got up to get his tray a small piece of paper came under the door. He grabbed the paper and his tray at the same time then went and sat back on the bed.

Uncovering the tray he was met by a 5star meal. Looking up at the door to see if anybody was watching, he quickly read the paper. Do not eat the grits they have NANObots in it so they can control you. Juan sat there for a second thinking about what else they could have done to his food,before he got it. He took a deep breath then dug in. He ate everything but the grits, then sat the tray back into the flap.

As he turned around he knew that it had to be a better way. Being stuck in a cell for 13 years, he knew that he wasn't about to spend no more of his life like this. His mind went to racing as he paced the floor. Trying to come up with a way out but still be there for his brother.Then it hit him "they said that I can go as I please once they got done running tests. So it's no need to break out I'll just tell them I'm ready to leave". As soon as he made that statement the tray flap shut. Juan jumped from being startled. He quickly looked back at the door, but didn't see anyone. All he heard was footsteps running away from the door.

Juan knew that it was going to be hard to leave that place freely.

No later than twenty minutes the door came open. A guard took two steps in the room and told Juan to come with him. As he followed behind the guard, he noticed that they weren't headed to the training area. "Excuse me homie where we going"

"Mr.Bush wants to talk to you"

"Good because I need to talk to him to"

Arriving at the office Juan was buzzed in. As he walked into the office he took a good look around. The closer he got to the desk,

Mr.Beans slowly turned around.

"Mr.Johnson it's a pleasure to meet with you this morning but we have a problem"

"Yeah we do"

"Ok do you want to go first? Well never mind I'll go. I was just told that you wanted to leave"

"I knew that motherfucker was ease dropping, but yea I can't be here"

"And why is that Mr.Johnson?"

"Man you got a brother all locked in the room like I'm back in prison. But you say we can go and come as we please"

"Well Mr.Johnson we still have more test to run on you"

"Shid we gone have to work something out because I ain't staying another night in that cell"

Mr.Beans stood up out of his chair and leaned on the desk.

"What do you mean you're not going to stay another night? You gone do what I tell you to do, you belong to me now"

"Man you got me fucked up standing there looking like a can of baked beans in that brown ass suite. You can't keep me here, I only came back for my brother"

"You have no choice Mr.Johnson"

As soon as Juan turned to walk out the door, the door came flying open and guards rushed in. He looked back at Mr.Beans and shook his head. Quickly making up his mind if he was going to comply or not. Juan took off running. Up rooting the flooring where his foot was planted. As he went through the crowd of guards a loud siren went off.

While running through the hallways trying to find an exit, guards continued to appear. Taking them out as they came for him. He knew that it would only be a matter of time before they cornered him. Checking all of the doors as he ran through the halls. Juan ran inside a training room. With all of the lights out he took a second to rest, until he came up with a new plan.

Within seconds the doors locked and the lights came on. Juan was surrounded with no way out. As he looked around he noticed that it wasn't guards this time around, it was the experiments. Everyone that they had mutated came to join the fight. They stood around him showing off their skills. Ready to zap him with fire balls and whatever else their gifts were. Feeling and knowing that he had no way out, Juan took a deep breath and got into his fighting stance. Mumbling under his breath that he wasn't going out without a fight. Everyone parted like the red sea as Pharaoh and Mr.Beans came walking through.

"There's no way out Mr. Johnson"

"Look I don't know what kind of games y'all playing but I don't want in"

"It's too late, you are already in"

"Pharaoh you ain't gone do nothing about this?"

"Can't you tell Mr.Johnson your brother is on our side"

"What have you done to my brother?" "Nothing but some good old science Mr.Johnson, just good old science"

"Yo Pharaoh you need to snap out of it and help me out here"

"It's ok lil bro just come with us and be apart of something great"

"Man fuck all........"

Before he could finish his statement, he was hit with a stun gun. Making him drop completely to the ground. Awakening to the cold feeling of chains around his wrist and ankle. Juan gave them a little tug just to see if he was dreaming. And within seconds two nurses and a guard came rushing in the room.

"It's ok sir, just lay back down"

"Fuck that! Let me out of these chains and where the hell is my brother?"

"Uh.....uh who is your brother?"

"Dr.Johnson and he needs to get here ASAP" "I'm sorry but he is with another patient at the moment"

Juan looked at her with a look as if he wanted to kill her. His body temperature heated up with each second that he stared at her. Turning completely red the madder he got, the hotter he became. As the cuffs slowly began to melt, the nurses took off running out the room. Screaming for Dr.Johnson to come help. Meanwhile the guard tried to stun him all over again, but it only sat him on fire. His body heat was getting too hot. He was beginning to set things on fire. As he stepped out into the hallway, he saw Pharaoh running towards him. Stopping mid ways Pharaoh told Juan to calm down.

"And why should I do that you left me out there by myself"

"No Juan I didn't"

"Yes you did, you letting them treat me like them other motherfuckers"

"Bro I told you to follow my lead but you not listening"

"This is what I get for coming here trying to save yo ass"

"Listen I'm trying to help you get to the point where you can control your gift at will and not out of anger"

"Look like I'm doing just fine without you big bro!"

"Juan please calm down so I can talk to you, I can't stand up under all of this heat your putting off"

Juan looked at Pharaoh and shook his finger at him. "Boy you lucky I love you big bruh"

Juan stated as he cooled down. Pharaoh began walking towards him as he changed back to his normal color. Then extended his arms looking for a hug. Juan smacked his teeth as he took a deep breath, then embraced his brother with a hug. Feeling a small prick hit right shoulder, Juan began to get sleepy. "What did you do to me?"

"Sorry lil bro I had to do what's necessary, it's just a lil morphine it will wear off"

"Why are you helping......"

Juan passed out in the middle of his sentence. Pharaoh adjusted himself so he could hold just until they made it to the wheelchair. After gently placing him inside of the wheelchair, Pharaoh pushed him down the hall.

6

Popping up awakening from the morphine. Juan looked around to see where he was and noticed that he was in a different room. It was ten times better than his last room. But that still didn't put him at ease. Juan got out of bed and went straight for the door. He turned around and gave it three good kicks. He waited for a second then kicked it three more times. On the last kick someone came over the small speaker box that was built inside the wall. "How can I help you Mr.Johnson?"

"Hell you can start by letting a nigga out of here then we can go from there"

"Well Mr.Johnson someone is on their way right now to talk to you"

"Man here y'all go with all this talking shit, I just want to be free"

"Mr.Johnson this is all to help you, why won't you let us help you?"

The sliding window opened up on the door and there stood Pharaoh looking inside. Juan frowned up his face out of disappointment from seeing his brother.

"Man what the fuck you want?" "Lil bro just hear me out"

"Don't lil bruh me and you been letting these white forks have they way with me"

"No I haven't Juan, your just so stubborn your not even trying to listen to me"

"Man that's cause you keep telling me that you can't talk, but yo ass show enough talking now" Pharaoh dropped his folder of documentations on the floor and went to pick them up. Just so he could slide Juan another note under the door. As he stood back up he advised Juan to put that somewhere safe until later. Hearing footsteps coming down the hallway, Pharaoh quickly changed topics. He began to talk about some of his lab work. And within seconds he caught a slight migraine.

Holding his head with both of his hands as he took a deep breath. Letting out a small grunt as he shook his head out of pain. As he removed his hands he rubbed the right side of his face. Then lifted his head back up and looked Juan dead in his eyes.

"Boy what the fuck wrong with you?" "Nothing I just need to get back to work"

"Aye Dr.Johnson your not suppose to be down here"

"Umm I know Ms.Kite, I'm leaving right now" "And what is it that you need Mr.Johnson?"

"Man what the hell y'all got going on and what the fuck y'all done did to my brother?"

"Well Mr. Johnson I can't talk to you about Dr.Johnson that's classified, but what I can tell you is that your blood is unique, its pure,it's like we never seen before"

"Man mix me with that bullshit, me and my brother got the same blood"

"That may be true but yours is so different. If we wouldn't have drew blood when the accident happen we would never been able to run so many test"

"Ok well if you know that I'm so special then that mean you know that I can break out of here at anytime right"

The intercom made a noise and Mr. Beans began talking.

"Now you don't want to do that Mr. Johnson think about your brother!"

"So you've been listening to us this whole time?"

"Not only have I been listening, I've been watching you to. So you might want to think about next time you see your brother"

The intercom went off and the nurse shut the window. Juan pounded the door out of frustration and anger, leaving a big dent in it.

As he turns around he wipes the tear out of his eye. Feeling like it's happening all over again. The incarceration and let down of himself and the family. Juan took a seat on the bed and took a deep breath.

As he looked around the room, he remembered the note that Pharaoh slid under the door. Juan stuck his hand into his pants and pulled the note off his hip. Then laid across the bed with his back towards the door, as if he was resting. Then begin to read the note.

"Lil bro the reason why I can't talk to you how I would like to is because I slipped and ate the food one day and didn't know that it had Nanobots in it. Everyone that works here is infected with them. And he has been controlling and watching my every move since you came to see me. The Nanobods have an off and on switch to them so he can watch whoever he wants to. But I'm trying to find a way to get them out of my system. That's why I asked you to follow my lead. Once I find that way we can take them down. And I also found out that the radioactive chemicals affect your body differently. Whatever that wasn't in your body at the time of the accident, your body want let it in.Unless you let your guard down, but even then your body will realize what's going on then it will take over. But it's a must that you learn how to fully control your powers. Love Big bro"

While destroying the letter his mind went to racing. He begin to think about all the things that his mother was telling him. And on top of that what Pharaoh told him in the letter. Laying there looking up at the ceiling as his mind continued to race, Juan slowly drifted off.

"Aye Juan you feel like playing super heroes?" "Yeah but this time I want to create my powers as I go"

"Ok cool, well this time I want to be a brainy yak that can multiply himself"

"Ok so who are we going after?" "Umm....A mad scientist, no wait a bank robber, no both"

"Ok"

Running around the house pretending to be super heroes. Virginia came storming down the stairs after hearing something shatter. Pharaoh quickly moved away from the broken flower vase. Leaving Juan standing there by himself as if he did it. "Boys what in the hell are y'all doing down here?" she questioned as she came down the last few steps. She looked at Pharaoh then looked in the opposite direction, to see Juan standing there next to the broken glass.

"JUAN I'M GOING TO BEAT YO ASS ! " Juan jumped up out of his sleep looking around. Feeling relaxed because it was only a dream.He began laughing to himself, because he couldn't help but realize after all these years, he was still afraid of his mother's ass whippings. Laying back down, he began thinking about his dream and realized that, that was the key to all of this. He jumped out of bed and ran over to the intercom. Impatiently pressing the button hoping that someone would answer. Mr.Beans finally answered "Yes

Mr. Johnson how may I help you"

"Look you win ok, I just want out of here"

"How do I know you want try to escape again" "Mr. Beans if I wanted to I would have be gone and besides that my brother is here"

"Well yea you do have a valid point there and what do you mean you want out of here?"

"I just want to get out this room and so I can be able to move around"

"So are you telling me that you're ready to play team ball now Mr. Johnson?"

"I guess I am sir"

"Well that means training and following by the rules"

"You're the Boss! If that's what you want"

"Ok then welcome to the team, but I'm still going to keep close watch on you"

"That's cool, so when are you going to let me out of here?"

Waiting for Mr. Beans to reply, Juan realized that it had got very quiet. "Hello! Hello Mr. Beans are you there?" Juan waited a few more seconds before walking off. As soon as he sat down on his bed the door opened. Six guards ran in and pointed their guns directly at him. Juan raised his arms and hands in the air. "Man what is all this for, I just made a peace treaty with your boss. I'm one of you now"

Mr. Beans walked in clapping his hands. Juan gave him a little mug then took his hands out the air.

"Man how are we going to be a team and you pulling stunts like this?"

"Well Mr. Johnson I just wanted to make sure you wasn't playing me"

"Nah but you pull a move like that again I'm going to say fuck it all"

"No No No it's no need for that. So you were saying that you wanted out of this room right?" "Yeah I want out, at least let me hit the town for a night to relax my mind and i'll show back up bright and early"

"Mr.Johnson we got to take baby steps here to make sure we are on the same page"

"I'm telling you we don't have to go through all of that, ok just let me hit the hallways then"

"Ok now we are talking. Look I'm going to allow you to move around here like the veterans that's been here for a while" "Ok cool I can deal with that"

Juan smiled and walked off. Hearing Mr.Beans call out his name as he continued to walk further away from him. Knowing in his head that everything had to count from that point on.

7

3 months later......

"Damn time has flew by and who's to think I would be at the top around here. I got my own crew now. And I can control my powers better than ever.I really can get used to this. "Juan thought to himself as he put gear on. Looking in the mirror checking himself out before leaving the room."Damn I look good in black"

As he walked through the hallways, he kept an eye out for Pharaoh. Not seeing him inside none of the laboratories was unusual. Juan asked one of the nurses if she had seen him. She just shook her head No and kept working. He politely waved at her and walked off. Knowing that he would run into him sometime or another.

Juan made his way to his favored training room, so he could get his morning work out in. As he hit the lights he was startled by Pharaoh standing there in the dark.

"Nigga you can't be scaring a brother like that, I almost blasted yo ass!"

"Shh boy you too loud!! Look it's time" "Time for what?"

"Juan I found it, we no longer have to be here"

"Oh shit that's what you're talking about. Ok well cool because I wanted to tell you something anyways"

"What is it because we have to make it quick" "Ok do you remember how we used to act like superheroes back in the day?"

"Yeah but what are you getting at?"

"Well that's how I was able to control my powers.Every power that I acted like I had back then I have now. And I believe if you was to give yourself the treatment you will be just like me"

"Umm....you might be onto something"

"I had a dream a while back about us as kids acting as superheroes"

"Why didn't you bring this to my attention sooner?"

"I had to find myself and I was following your lead"

"Ok look we never had this talk and i'll let you know when the time is right"

Pharaoh slid out of the training room and went on his way. Juan began to smile as he started his warm up. Thinking to himself that the time has finally come for him to do what he does best. And that was to get into some gangsta shit. As the time passed people began to come inside. And Juan stopped using his powers and worked more on hand to hand combat. Over hearing people talking about how Mr.Beans has been sending people out on missions/trial runs made him wonder.

He grabbed his towel and threw it around his neck then walked out of the training area. Wiping the sweat off of his face as he exited the room, he bumped into Gabby. Apologizing before he even saw who it was.

"Boy you knew what you was doing"

"Nah I really wasn't trying to, but I see that's the only way a brother can get close to you" "Nah you just ain't tried hard enough"

"See I knew deep down you really liked me" "Maybe but that doesn't mean I wasn't gonna make you put in so work"

"Oh you mine now you shouldn't have told me that"

"Boy bye....take yo silly butt on somewhere" "Yeah i'll catch you later" Juan said as he rubbed his chin hairs smiling, while dancing backwards. Gabby started blushing and he knew that he had her from that moment. Turning around so he could see where he was going, he quickly detoured to Mr.Beans office. Arriving in front of Mr.Beans office, it was three guards standing there. Which was unusual for that many guards to be at his office at one time, unless it was a code red.

"hey what's going on... is it a code red?"

"Nah! The boss man just want more security around"

"oh well can you let him know that I'm out here"

"Sure thing Mr. Johnson, you know you always welcome"

The guard got on his radio and

Informed Mr. Beans that Mr. Johnson was on his way in. As he entered the room Mr. Beans set up in his chair. "My main man Juan, what can I do for you?"

"Is it true that you've been sending people outside the facility?"

"where you hear that from"

"now if I tell you that then it makes me a rat, but is it true?"

"Well yeah it's true but before you say anything let me explain"

"Man it's no needs I'm not your bitch, I just thought we was better than that" "Yeah we are but I have to do some test runs and I wanted your mission to be more special"

"Wait what do you mean mission?"

Mr.Beans got quiet as he stared at Juan for a few seconds before telling him that he was slowly trying to take over the world.

"Man I knew you were planning that shit. You just looked like one of those motherfukers that got picked on your whole life and now that you got money you want the world to feel your pain."

"Well you are right and I got an army to help me do it"

"Hell I ain't mad at you just throw me a flew m's so me and the family will be str8"

"See Mr.Johnson you are the key to all of this" "Whatcha you talkin bout Willis?! I ain't got shit to do with this,this yo plan"

"Nice Gary Coleman joke but Juan you are the muscle. You are stronger than all the rest. So I sent them out to warm the world up for what to come"

"And what's that because like I said your plan not mine"

"Now Juan your acting like your not a team player"

"Yea you are right so what is it that you want me to do?"

"I'll tell you when the time is right just be ready" "I'm always ready, you know that," Juan stated as he began walking backwards through the door. As he turned around and went out the door,he heard Beans call for one of the guards to come inside the office. He knew that he was going to be trailed for the rest of the evening.

Meanwhile Pharaoh was back at the lab,doing last minute testing. He knew that the cure worked for his D.N.A perfectly,but he wanted to be able to help some of the others. Rolling back and forth between lab stations and hopping on and off the computers.

Hearing keys rattle inside of the door before it opened, Pharaoh quickly removed the small bottle of cure. Cuffing it inside of his hand not having time to hide it anywhere else, Dr.Phenomenon walked right over to him.

"Hey handsome,what are you up to" she spoke with her Korean accent

"You know me working hard trying to come up with something new"

"Yes you do work like a mad scientist at times" Dr.Phenomenon stated as she walked out. Pharaoh quickly slid the bottle inside of his pocket. "Hey Doc, remind me to show you something later." Pharaoh said as he headed for the door.

"Bout time you"

"Huh?! What did you just say?" "Nothing I just said ok"

Dr.Phenomenon said as she stood there smiling at Pharaoh. Pharaoh knew she said something slick because she was always hitting on him. But he didn't have the time to play her little game. He reached inside of the glass storage cabinet and grabbed a syringe. Placing it inside of his pocket then walked out the door. Looking around to see if anyone noticed him coming out of the room before he moved on.

Taking a deep breath to calm down, after realizing that he only had to move like he does everyday. As he headed towards the transformation room he bumped into Gabby.

"Hey have you seen my brother?"

"Not since earlier, when he was coming out of the training room"

"Oh ok I haven't seen him all day, if you see him tell him I'm looking for him"

"Yeah sure"

Pharaoh smiled then kept it moving. Knowing that she would go find Juan just because he said something to her about him. Arriving at the first treatment room that they ever had. Pharaoh went inside and locked the doors. Pulling out the syringe and the antidote.

He filled the syringe to 3fl oz., then injected into his veins. While waiting for the antidote to kick in, he turned on the transformation machine. Making sure that he had everything that he needed when the time was right.

He felt a squirming sensation inside of his stomach and knew it was time. He grabbed the control button then sat inside the chair. Strapping himself down around the waist, then putting his mouthguard in. Closing his eyes he counted to three, then hit the button. The machine started it up and injected him in three different places, with three different forms of radioactive elements.

Button-down on a mouthguard Ester chemical elements took over his body. Rocking from side to side trying his best to endure the pain, as he the arms of the chair. Conjuring up enough willpower to unwrap himself. Pharaoh stood up out of the chair and fell face first. Laying there for a second before pushing himself up.

Leaning up against a small medal table, before using it to pull himself up. Pharaoh staggered out the door and down the hall. Finding a cut to hide in as he got some rest. The transformation was too much for him at that time, all he wanted to do was rest.

Meanwhile Juan had been flirting with

Gabby until he overheard one of the nurses asking if they had seen Dr.Johnson. He looked back at them to see who it was, then Gabby blurted out "oh I forgot to tell you that your brother was looking for you"

"And when was this?"

"This was after you bumped into me earlier" Juan paused for a moment then took off.

Running through the Halls checking every lab room, until he found Pharaoh Lane off to the side. Quickly dashing into the cut and she called out Pharaoh's name. Shaking Pharaoh to make sure he was still alive. As he began to wake, Juan helped him sit up

"Bro what's wrong?"

"I'll explain later but for now you have to get us out of here"

"Hell I thought you would never ask"

Juan lifted Pharaoh up and tossed them over his shoulders. Making his way through the halls trying to find a good exit point.

They were spotted by one of the guards. Juan took off running, not giving the guard a chance to stop him or ask any questions. And before he knew it the alarm was going off, and the hallways began to become flooded with guards. Every hallway they turned down had guards on it. Finally fighting his way to a hallway they had a parking lot view, Juan sat Pharaoh down.

Taking a deep breath exhaling as he punched the wall, putting a big hole into it. Picking Pharaoh off the ground, guards started coming around the corner. As they released fire Juan ran through the hole with Pharaoh. Running at supersonic speed trying to get as far away from the agency as possible. While running he passed by a gas station and noticed that someone had left their door open.

He turned around and hopped inside of the car. Slapping the car in Drive then smashing the gas. As he fishtailed out of the gas station, he looked over at Pharaoh. And he was sound asleep. Juan knew that whatever he had done was on him heavy. 15 minutes later they arrived at their mom's house. Juan woke pharaoh up by trying to get him out of the car. "Juan we can't be here"

"What do you mean this moma house"

"I know that but we are not safe here. We have to get moma and get out of here. I have a safe spot we can go up in the mountains."

"Ok I'll be right back"

Juan took off inside the house. Searching it from top to bottom but not seeing their mother nowhere in sight. Until you heard the back door open, he quickly ran into the kitchen. Seeing his mother walk through the door brought a smile to his face. Before she could say a word, he told her that they had to go. Quickly picking her up and running out of the house.

He put her on the back seat and jumped back behind the wheel.

Smashing the gas spitting grass everywhere. All he heard was his mother yelling about her grass. As they headed for the expressway, a fleet a black SUVs and cars was headed in the direction they just came from. Juan hit the expressway headed north.

8

Arriving at the small but cozy looking log cabin, Juan tapped Pharaoh to make sure they were at the right spot.

"Yeah this is it help me out the car"

"You had this place all this time and didn't tell me" Ms.Virginia questioned

"Yea ma this is where I use to come them days no one could reach me"

As Juan helped Pharaoh out of the car,while Ms.Virginia was still going on about not being invited to his log cabin. Juan helped Pharaoh to the steps,then lent him up against the house. Pharaoh slides back a piece of wood and begin punching in a code. Once he was done the wood slid back in place and the door opened. All the lights came on inside of the cabin as soon as Pharaoh stuck his feet inside.

"Damn bruh when you have this built?"

"Well I had some help from the agency when I was an intern"

"What the fuck?! Bruh how stupid can you be for being us here. You know they gone come here"

"Just chill lol brother they want be coming out here because they don't know nothing about this place"

"What?! Man you aint making no sense" "See I had transferred some money to a dummy account and then erased the transactions. Everything has been covered up so we are good."

Juan stood there shaking his head with a silly little smirk on his face. Knowing that his brother wasn't a goodie two shoes after all. Then it dawned on him that he had to get rid of the car. He took off out of the cabin and jumped into the car. Taking the car to the nearest gas station and parked it on the side of the road. Popping the hood then taking off back down the road to the cabin.

As he arrived back at the cabin,he realized that he didn't have a key to get inside the house. And Pharaoh didn't give him the code. He stood there knocking on the door waiting for them to answer,but no one came. He walked to the back of the cabin and looked inside the window. He could see Pharaoh laying down on the couch,but that only made him wonder where his mom was.

As soon as he was about to walk away from the window,he spotted her coming out of the restroom. Tapping on the window to get her attention. Ms.Virginia quickly looked at the window, then frowned her face at Juan. Wondering what he was doing in the back of the house. As she let him in through the back door, she asked him what he was doing back there.

He just looked at her and walked right past her. Feeling like that was a crazy question to ask him. As he kept walking he gave himself a tour around the house. Picking out a room to crash in, Juan laid across the bed and fell asleep.

Meanwhile,while they were safe and cozy at the cabin, Mr.Beans and his crew had torn their house apart. Looking for anything that could lead him to where they would go to hide. Seeing torn up grass and tire marks,he knew that they weren't coming back no time soon. Mr.Beans ordered for the hounds to be turned loose. Calling them over to make them smell the tracks.

The hounds picked up the scent immediately and took off. Everybody quickly loaded backup to follow the dogs. As they got closer the scent was fading away. And the dogs kept going around the same spot.

Frustratingly rubbing his head then banging on the hood of the car.

The order for the house we put up. As a loaded back up and hit the road they passed by the car on the opposite side of the road. Mr. Beans looked at the car long and hard, feeling like that could have been his key. Changing his mind and going with his gut feeling, he made them turn around.

Looking inside of the car to see if he could spot anything that would link the car to Juan or Pharaoh. The hounds started barking, so Mr.Beans ordered for them to let one hound out. Circling around the vehicle trying to pick up a scent. The hound jumped up on the door and started braking. The guard opened the door.

The hound rushed inside of the car,making the door hit the guard in the face. The hound sat behind the wheel braking. Mr.Beans knew that they were somewhere close. Pulling the dog back out the car to see if he would pick up the trail again. But it only kept going back to the car. Spotting a gas station not too far from the car gave him an idea.

Once they arrived at the gas station, Mr.Beans took six guards inside with him.

"How are you doing sir? You wouldn't happen to know who car that is would you"

"No sir I sure don't but I have a car I can sell you"

"Ummm where is your security system at?" " Now wait just a minute that's private information"

Mr. Bean gave the head signal and three guards took off searching the store. The other three apprehended the old man. As they continued their search customers came in and turned right back around. Calling 911 as they ran back to their cars. Finally finding the security cameras receiver they check to see if any camera had the car in sight.

"Wait go back"

As they rewind the tape and played it back. The only thing they could see was a small portion of the car. They only made him more frustrated, being so close but so far at the same time. Letting the store manager go then began to walk out the door. Seeing the cops had the place surrounded made Mr.Beans smile. "it's showtime boys"

As they walked out of the store, the police yelled over the loudspeaker "Freeze". One of the guards ran up and started shooting icicles out of her hands. Another one gave them a windstorm. Blowing them and their cars to the other side of the parking lot. And as they loaded up another guard spray fire on the ground blocking the police in as they made their getaway.

9

The next day Juan was awakening to the sound of the News. Slowly getting up on the side of the bed, he looked at the clock. Seeing that it was a little after 11, he knew that it was about time to get up anyways. As he stood inside the bathroom getting himself together, he heard the News reporter saying something about breaking News. He quickly rinsed his mouth out and took off out of the bathroom.

Standing in front of the t.v watching the reporter and the camera man hide behind cars,as they gave their report. Seeing that Mr.Beans has unleashed a new group of experiments. And they were not too far from them. And that only meant two things to Juan. That they were close on their trail and that they couldn't hide forever. And that brought him to the realization that Pharaoh wasn't on the couch.

He began to look around the house for Pharaoh and their mother. Not seeing them nowhere in sight, he ran to the window. Looking outside the house,he didn't see them in the front so he checked the back. Still nowhere to be found. So he yelled out their names as he looked out the back window. Hoping to get some type of response.

But still no answer. "This some bullshit,they could have at least left a brother a note saying something." Juan spoke to himself as he looked through the refrigerator for something to eat. Forgetting that Pharaoh hasn't been there in years. He slammed the frigerator door out of frustration.

And noticed that the floor had moved back some, and a light

was shining under the floor. That made him wonder if it was a secret room built in or if it was the basement. He pushed the refrigerator back some more and saw a flight of stairs. He cautiously walked down the stairs. Standing at the bottom of the stairs, Juwan looked around. It was a whole nother house down there, with glass walls.

Juan took a few steps up and pushed on the door. A picture of Pharaoh projected across the glass.

"So you finally woke up"

"yeah thank you guys for leaving the TV up so loud"

"oh sorry about that"

"Umm are you going to let me in or what?" "Oh yea right!"

Pharaoh buzzed him in,and Juan gave himself a mini tour as he made his way to Pharaoh.

"Aye bruh have you seen the news?" "Yeah that's why I couldn't rest no longer" "Ok so that mean you have came up with a plan"

"Not as of yet but I'm working on a few things" "Ok let me see what u got. Oh but first where is moma?"

"Oh she is in the other room watching tv" "What?! How many rooms do you have in this cabin"

"Ummm just say we have enough room to do whatever we want"

Juan looked around and couldn't believe what he was hearing. He could see that it was pretty big but not how he was talking. Pharaoh looked at him and smiled,then told him that they were just in the laboratory.

"Damn bruh you had this planned out didn't you?"

"Naw not really I just took a leap on the wild side and everything worked out"

"Ok Mr.Wildside where do we go from here?" "Well I'm glad you asked"

Pharaoh begin showing and telling Juan all the ideas that he had done so far. And the more he talked the more hungry Juan became. Stopping Pharaoh in mid sentence,to let him know that they had to get some food in the house, before he could do anything.

"Don't worry the groceries have been delivered already and ma is cooking as we speak"

"Man what the hell is you talking about. Moma ain't been no damn where,and I ain't heard no damn door bell ring"

"Little bro that's why I love the technology and science"

"Well nigga I'm going to eat I'll be back when I'm done"

Juan took off back out of the lab. Thinking to himself that his brother had done went crazy.

Or he might be just as crazy for believing that it's food up stairs and he had just come from up there. As he begins to walk up the steps the floor begin to retract. And the aroma of food being cooked hit his nose. He couldn't believe it.

Seeing his moma standing over the stove cooking brought a smile to his face. He didn't know which one made him happier at the moment. Coming up on the side of his mother and giving her a kiss on the cheek.

"Ma how did you get all of this food without leaving the house?"

"Boy Wal-Mart got this new system where you can order online and they deliver"

"Oh damn Wal-Mart got the game on smash. Well how did you get up stairs and I didn't see you"

"Your brother got this place set up with all kind of special treats"

"Well why he aint gave me a tour"

"In do time Juan but for now here eat up" Setting Juan's plate down in front of him then hitting a little green button that she had on her apron. Waiting for Pharaoh to come up the stairs before she sat down as well. She gave him a few minutes then hit the button again. Figuring that he had got suck into his work she went ahead and ate with Juan.

15 minutes later they were done eating and Juwan was back downstairs. Standing in front of the glass door with Pharaoh's plate in his hand. Waiting for him to open the door he noticed some movement into different parts of the lab. Thinking that someone had broken into the lab, he began to heat up the door so he could go inside the lab.

But before he could actually touch the door

Pharaoh popped up on the glass.

"Oh sorry little bro I got caught up in working" "Ok cool let me in"

As he entered back into the lab, he noticed that Pharaoh was everywhere. He had multiplied himself. Juan's head was on a constant swivel, looking for the real Pharaoh. He yelled out Pharaoh's name hoping that he would answer. But every last one of his clones answered. Juan just shook his head knowing that he wasn't going to get anywhere like that.

"Look bruh I got your food right here, so come out of hiding or whatever you call this and come get it"

All of Pharaoh's clones begin to retract themselves as Pharaoh begins to walk towards Juan. Pharaoh walked up and took the plate straight out of Juan's hand.

"Yo bruh you were right"

"About what? And don't you want to eat first?"

"I can do both. I'm super excited right now. But you were right about everything yeah I wanted to be when we were kids, I really have those powers now"

"See what I tell you but we just have to find I what to do with them now"

"Don't worry I'm on top of that, check this out" Pharaoh multiplied himself one time, so you can finish eating. Taking Juan to the back to show him the new things he was working on.

Showing him two different types of vehicles that he designed just for him.

"Pharaoh I can move in supersonic speed what do I need with a car or a motorcycle"

"okay you might be right so we will come back to that. Now check this out"

Pharaoh went back to the first plans in gadgets. Showing Juan how they could get back inside of the company and save those who haven't been changed. Juan listens to his plans and realizes that it wouldn't work. He needed to make a few changes for the plan to go that smooth. He shared a few ideas with Pharaoh and he went into thinking mode.

2 minutes later the real pharaoh walked up and told you one to follow him. He took him into another part of the lab, where a machine was sitting in the middle of the floor.

"What is this for?"

"well I just put it together this morning and I'm about to show, you just step right here"

"Man you don't even know if it works"

"Oh it works, I tried it out already. Oh and by the way what is your favorite color?"

"Green is my favorite color"

"Okay cool I want to mix it up just a little bit, but go ahead and step inside"

Juan stepped inside the machine and turned around to face Pharaoh. And it dawned on him, what in the hell did his favorite color have to do with this machine. But before he could ask Pharaoh the door closed on him. Infrared lights lit up his body, scanning him from head to toe. The infrared lights shut off and the bottom of the machine started to move. As it worked its way up,it shot out genetically enhanced fabric that was stocking itself together to make a full body suite.

Once the machine was done Juan stepped out in his custom suit. Green on the outside with a thick black strip down the middle, with gold fabric throughout its entire suit.

"Bruh I like the suit and all but what does the S with the crown around it means?" "Supreme"

"Oh my middle name but it's like I'm hitting off of Superman"

"See little bro that's where you're wrong. Your S symbolizes Supreme being and his S was really and H for hope. He was passing out hope to the world but my brother we are the world"

"I never thought about it like that"

"Sometimes someone has to open your eyes to things that's been in front of you the whole time"

"Yeah that's true"

"Besides, you will be better than Superman, once you get the hang of things. Now follow me."

Juan smiled as he followed Pharaoh, not knowing that his big brother thought so highly of him. As they entered into another room, Juan's eyes got bigger as he looked around in awww.

"Damn bruh this is a mean set up you got here" "Yeah I actually design it for you because I know how you like to play with guns but now it's a training area for everything"

As Juan continued to look around he stepped across the training line and unknowingly activated the training ground. Hologram targets popped up and began shooting at him. He kept walking until he started getting hit by the target's weapon. "Yo Pharaoh tell me why am I feeling these shots bro?"

"Even though they are holograms your suit is designed to interact with your attacks. So if you get hit you will feel the impact"

"Why didn't you tell me?"

"Because I wanted every moment of your training to be as real as it could be"

"So you telling me this fancy suit ain't prof?" "The suite is designed to do whatever you can do. So whatever power you have the suit is made for it."

Juan shook his head and cracked his knuckles smiling as he walked back on to the training platform. But this time a hologram of himself popped up.

"Oh shit thats me"

"Yeah that's you but with the combat skill of a lot of great warriors downloaded to him like Bruce Lee,Mike Tyson, Shaka Zulu, and etc…" "I got skills but damn, you trying to get a brother beat up!"

"There are all kinds of fighting styles and skills to help you become the greatest hero alive. Well enjoy, I have work to do."

As he walked off Juan looked at the hologram then looked at Pharaoh and shook his head. Having no idea where he was coming up with all of this.

10

Later that evening Juan had finished his training for the day. As he exited out the same door Pharaoh did he noticed that it only took him into another room. This room was set up with a big monitor screen, and a desk with buttons and keypads. He continued to walk until he exited out of the following room which only led him to another room. Which didn't make any sense to him.

So an idea popped into his head. He took off running in supersonic speed, giving himself a mini tour of everything while finding his way back to the glass room. As he walked back through the glass room Pharaoh and his clones were hard at work.

"Aye bro check this out"

Am I talking to a clone or is it really you?" "It's me, fool but look at this I have made the antidote better. It not only cures you so he can't control you but it cures from the transformation and heals you completely."

"Okay Inspector Gadget, while you're getting it all put together, I'm going to relax I have been on the go since I've been free"

"Now wait just a minute take this with you" "What is this?"

"it's a transmitter"

"So you're tracking me now!?"

"Yeah some what but it's also so I can communicate with you"

"Man you're taking this to far, just call me on the cell like a normal person"

Juan handed him back the transmitter and walked up the stairs.

Feeling a little bit of let down and hurt Pharaoh went back inside of the lab. Meanwhile back D.N.A Mr.Beans was still in a frenzy. He lost his head doctor and his powerfulest experiment. He began to make the ones he had work & train harder. Knowing that Pharaoh and Juan had to be stopped because they knew too much. He didn't want the company to go under.

Knocking everything off his desk out of frustration before putting his head down. On another note Juan had found himself a nice little night club, in Blue Ridge Ga. It was different from what he was used to, but anything was better than being stuck in the lab. As the pop music played people rushed to the dance floor. Juan walked over to the bar and ordered a shot of Apple Henessy. As he sipped his drink he scanned the area for a nice spot to post up at.

As he bobbed his head to the music he looked for a pretty little thing he could push up on. Spotting a nicely tanned white chick on the dance floor going white girl crazy. He thought it would be fun to get on the dance floor and go crazy with her. Quickly downing his drink then headed to the dance floor. He stepped in front of her and started doing what she was doing.

She looked over and smiled at him, then asked him what was he doing?

"I don't no I'm just trying to have some fun" "Oh I thought you liked my dancing"she spoke with a smile on her face

"Yeah I love it your the life of the party" "You're not from around here are you?" "Nah I'm from Atlanta"

"I thought so, you dress like from down there" "Is that a bad thing?"

"Not for me, but some of the forks up here don't like outsiders"

"Oh ok so that's my que" "What do you mean by that?" "Lets go over here and talk"

As soon as Juan turned around a black and white hillbilly was standing in his face. Juan looked them up and down before asking them if they could help them.

"You're an old city slicker aint cha?"

"Man what that got to do with y'all in my face, i'm here to enjoy myself"

"Well we don't like it when you old city slickers try to come steal our women away from us" "Man look I'm not trying to go there tonight I just came to have fun so excuse me"

Juan politely stepped to the side and went around them. As he headed back to where he was standing,he thought to himself that it was going to be a long night. He detoured and went back to the bar.

"Back already?!" "Yeah!"

"So what can I get you? Another Apple Henessy"

"Nah give me a Blue Motherfuker and a Longlsand IceTea"

"Oh ok coming right up"

As she sat the drinks on the bar Juan turned them up non stop. Her eyes got bucked, she cracked a smile.

"You must met Big Country and Big Bubba" "Yeah they blessed me with their present. But it's going to take more than that to run me out of here"

Juan paid the lady then walked back to his little post. Every now and then he would slide out on the dance floor,to get a dance in as the time passed by. Checking his watch to see what time it was he noticed it was 2am. He had been in there since 9. He finished up his last drink and decided to have a little fun with

Bubba and Country.

He took off running in supersonic speed passing by Bubba and Country while smacking the shit out of them. As he led back against the wall to watch their reaction. He thought it would be even funnier to splash them with their own drinks. He waited for a few minutes as they questioned each other. They both rubbed their face out of pain and confusion. He took off one more time.

This time he splashed them with their drinks and smacked them. They got up and went to brawling with each other and anybody that was near them. Trying to hold his laughs in as he pulled up to the bar for one more shot. "What can I get you?"

"I'll just have the Apple Henessy to take me out for the night"

"Ok one Apple Henessy coming up. Hope you enjoyed yourself"

"Yeah it was different but fun. But it's like the action is just starting"

"Yeah hon they are one strange team"

"Ok well take care" Juan stated as he paid the lady and started walking off. As he got closer to the other end of the bar,he spotted two chicks giggling as they looked at a US weekly magazine that had Ryan Reynolds on the front. He quickly looked around before changing into Ryan Reynolds. Walking close by the chicks to make sure they saw him.

"Hey sir have anybody ever told you that you look like Ryan Reynolds before"

"Yes all the time but they trip out when I tell them it's me"

"Oh my gosh shut up, it's you for real" "Yeah it's me the one and only"

"Are you about to leave?" "Yeah it's over for the night" "Can we come with you?" "How about I go with you two" "Oh god yes, sure why not"

They quickly grabbed their things and took his side. Not knowing that he could actually shape stiff into people surprised him. But he kept his cool and began to make them smile and laugh. They didn't even pay attention to the fact that they were getting into their car and not some fancy one. She just pulled out the parking lot and headed home.

11

The next morning Juan was awakened by the sound of his cell phone going off. He crawled out of bed trying not to wake the young ladies. He grabbed his things and tiptoed to the bathroom. Shutting the door behind him as he pulled out his phone.

"Bruh this better be an emergency with you blowing up the phone like this"

"Juan where are you? Have you seen the news?"

"No I haven't seen the news I was trying to sleep"

"Look wherever you are, turn on the TV. No matter of get back here asap"

Juan quickly put his pants and shoes on then came out of the bathroom. One of the chicks woke up as he turned the TV on. She looked at Juan and yelled "Aye who are you your not Ryan Reynolds"

"I know and your not Nicki Minaj or BeBe Rexon either but can you be quite so I can hear what their saying"

Turning back towards the TV while putting on his shirt. As he listened to the news, the chick woke up her homegirl. Asking her who was the black guy and what happened Ryan

Reynolds. Her friend didn't want to move, she kept waving her off. She was still buzzed from last night. And then out of nowhere she jumped up saying "Wait we had Ryan Reynolds here last night"

Juan looked back with a troubled looked on his face and knew it was time to get out of there. He took off running out of the bedroom and straight out the front door. Once he got a good little distance from the house he went into supersonic speed. High tailing it back to the cabin. Arriving back at the cabin he wasted no time going to the lab. Pharaoh was busy at work making last minute adjustments to the suit and other gadgets.

"So what's the plan bruh?"

"Well first thing first get dressed"

Juan grabbed the suit off of the mannequin and quickly put it on. Pharaoh walked back up to him and looked over the suit, then told him to him. As they began walking Pharaoh explained everything to him. Then told him to go get inside of the Supreme mobile.

"There you go biting off of Batman now" "What I tell you everybody copy someone but it's what you do to make it better or your own" "Ok Dr.King or should I say Malcolm"

Pharaoh just looked at him and shook his head as he walked into the control room. Juan entered the room where the Supreme mobile was and was amazed. It looked a whole lot better than it did on paper. Then candy apple paint and the chrome rims looked fly. Juan reached to open the door and noticed that the door didn't have a handle. The driver door didn't even open.

A hologram of Pharaoh appeared behind the driver seat. Pharaoh pointed to the passenger door. Juan looked around with a confused look on his face, before making his way to the other side. As he jumped inside the car it immediately started up. And Pharaoh came over the speaker, "There is no need for you to drive if your going to be hopping out that's why I built it this way"

The car began to move super fast and a passageway appeared out of nowhere. And before Juan knew it they were sliding out of the woods and onto the highway. Juan was still somewhat amazed, from the way the car turned out. All of the buttons that were lighting up,made him feel like a little kid. He wanted to see what they all did. As they arrived in downtown Finnin Ga, the police had the whole area blocked off.

Juan jumped out of the car while it was still rolling. By passing by the police cars at supersonic speed. Then stopped in the middle of the action, scanning the area to see how many experiments he was up against. A flaming car came flying through the air. All he could hear was yelling and screaming coming from every angle.

A police officer jumped on the loudspeaker telling him to get out the way. He looked back and gave him a thumbs up. That throws them for a loop. They didn't know where he came from or if he was one of them. Seeing Juan catch the flaming car and placing it on the ground,let them know that he was one of them.

They open fire on him. Juan took off in a zigzag motion in supersonic speed to throw them off. Popping up behind the lieutenant scaring the shit out of him, before telling him that he was on their side. Taking back off to defuse the situation. He tried to take the gentle approach first.

Juan stopped in front of the twins, and asked them to stop. The twins looked at him and smiled. Quickly shooting a fireball at his chest. Making him fly back a few feet before he regained his composure. Juan looked at them and dusted his suit off,then took off. Dodging fireballs as he made his way back over to them. Engaging into hand to hand combat with them.

Pharaoh came over the built-in speaker. Telling Juan that he needed to inject them with the cure.

"Ummm I'm kinda busy here don't you think" "Yeah but this is the best time to do it"

"Ok now how am I going to do that without the cure?"

"Don't worry, I made some modifications to the suit. It's a small button on the side of your left risk. If you tap it mini needles will come out your gloves, so when you hit them it will inject the cure inside of them."

"But what if I miss and hit myself?"

"It won't penetrate you suit so your good" One twin kicked low as the other one kicked high. Knocking him flat on his back,

then they released fire on him. As they stopped and the smoke cleared, they stood over him. Only to notice that he wasn't there anymore. They quickly begin to scan the area looking for him. Only to find him standing by a light pole.

Juan was fidgeting around trying to find the little button that Pharaoh told him about. Fireballs hit the side of the building. Juan took off rushing toward them. The twins grabbed each other's hand and a gastric fire dorm came over them. Melting everything that they came close to. The flames were getting hotter by the second. Juan adapted to the temperature.

Making his way inside of the dorm of fire. He quickly zipped over and grabbed one of the twins. Hitting him in the ribs injecting the serum inside of him. The dorm immediately stopped, and his sister went to comfort him. Seeing that he no longer had his power she began screaming. Holding him one arm as she released fire on Juan. Juan noticed that her power wasn't that strong anymore.

As the balls of fire hit his chest, he smiled and walked right up on her. Punching her right in the face. As the serum took over their body he left them laying on the ground to recover. The few officers that were still alive came from behind the building. Trying to stop Juan to just see what he goes by. He quickly yelled out Supreme before going into supersonic speed.

12

Feeling awesome from winning his first real battle. He went on ramping and raving about how explosives he was in the battle.

"Juan enough I seen the whole thing you need some work"

"Come on bruh, You know I was lit"

"Yeah you was nice but you took to long to get the situation under control, you could have lost a lot more lives"

"Damn bruh I feel like I did good for my first time you gotta let me get use to it"

"Juan I understand but there no time for that now hit the gym"

Juan looked at Pharaoh with his eyes squinted,as he thought inside his head that Pharaoh was some bullshit. He just walked out of the lab.

MEANWHILE

Mr.Beans was inside of his locator room, monitoring all of his experiments. Seeing that he had just lost the twins made him furious. He banged on the control board,then told everyone to get out. Stopping Dr.Phenomenon at the door.

"How much longer do you have before you break the code to his DNA?"

"Sir it's harder than you think"

"Well make it unhard we don't have time to waste"

"But sir his DNA is unusual,it's like it changes on its own. And we have to start all over." "Well fix it! Now dismiss yourself"

She clutched on to her folders tightly,as she quickly rushed out the room. Mr.Beans propped his feet up and stared at the monitors. Looking at his crew to see who he was going to send out for his next attack.

The next day was like deja vu. The news was flooded with attacks. Every channel Pharaoh turned on head breaking news. Starting from North Georgia all the way downtown Atlanta. In Roswell it looks as if they were having a hail storm. Large balls of ice and huge ice crystals were falling out of the sky.

And on the southside of Atlanta It's reporting of wild animals attacking people. And on Old National it was hard vibrations being felt. Small buildings were collapsing from the vibrations. Bankhead Highway was suffering from power outages and people were getting snatched up by a human bird. Downtown Atlanta was the worst, it was chaos everywhere. Pharaoh turned off the TV and sounded the alarm.

A buzzing sound went off in Juan's room before his bed dropped. Dropping him onto a slide. Falling into a pit of foam balls, Juan stood up and yelled out Pharaoh's name. As he climbed out of the pit Pharaoh was standing right there.

"No time to talk the city is under attack"

"Man fuck all of that,when did you have time to rig my bed?"

"Juan superheroes don't have time to sleep, now let's go"

"Fuck!! I didn't sign up for this shit gave me a minute"

Before Pharaoh could blink his eyes, Juan was back with his suit on.

"Ok what's going on in the city now?" "Get in and I'll tell you all about it" "Wait, you're going with me?"

"Yeah I'm sending a clone out with you this time"

Pharaoh cloned himself one time and sent them on their way. Pharaoh put the Supreme mobile into stealth mode,then hit the overdrive button. Sending them down the highway, making them arriving in Roswell in no time. Riding right into an ice storm. Big balls of hail and ice crystals were falling from everywhere.

Juan quickly jumped out of the Supreme mobile and scanned the area. Looking for any sign of where they could be. Cars were swerving in and out of traffic trying to dodge small cyclones. Looking up into the dark clouds Juan spotted someone on the rooftop. He knew with him standing there all cool and calm in the midst of everything, that was his target.

He took off running towards the building and got scooped up by a cyclone. Getting spent around for a few seconds before the cyclone disappeared. Falling out of the sky before he took back off towards the building. Going to supersonic speed to run up the side of the building. He was met by a female that hit him with a bomb of ice crystals. Sending him tumbling to the ground.

As Juan laid on the ground thinking to himself, how was he going to get close enough to them to take them out. They both came soaring off the roof. One rode down on a cyclone the other sled down on a large ice crystal. Quickly jumping to his feet, Juan was attacked. He was hit with bombs of ice crystals and mini worldwinds.

"I don't have time for this shit today" Juan thought to himself as he grounded himself. Making the lower half of his body weigh a ton. As he came out of the mini Cyclone he took off in a zigzag motion. Making it to them before they could make any adjustments. Choke slamming Cyclone to the ground while clipping the Ice Queen off her feet.

As they rolled around tussling on the ground. Cyclone used the force of the wind to slide away. Queens sprung to her feet and delivered two quick punches before releasing ice crystals out of her hands. As the ice crystals hit his chest they shattered. Cyclone roll back up in a tornado.

Jumping off the tornado with a flying knee. Juan kicked him out of the air but he was caught by another tornado. Queen rushed him with two ice swords that were attached to her hands. Juan backed up to dodge each swing she took at him. He remembered that all he had to do was harden himself, so the ice would break, he felt a little slow. Tapping himself upside the head, then took a deep breath to clear his mind.

He knew that he was still fighting in a stage of fear. As he opened his eyes he just took off. Rushing in on her forcing her to hand to hand combat. Not being able to withstand the brute strength that Supreme was putting out. Queen began to produce ice sculptures of herself at a rapid paste. Supreme broke through them as fast as she made them.

Reaching through the sculpture and grubbing her by suit. Pulling her in and injecting her with the cure. As soon as he injected her he was hit. Cyclone slide up on him without him even knowing. Regaining his composure he turned around looking for him.

Cyclone would disappear with the wind then pop back up inside of a tornado. Sending a gang of tornados to close Supreme into a circle. No matter how fast he would run to try to break free, he couldn't. Cyclone would pop up in a different tornado and deliver hits upon Supreme. Not being able to catch him before he would disappear.

Supreme caught on to his pattern. And soon as he tried to deliver his next hit, Supreme grabbed him and pulled him out of his shield of tornados. Hitting him with a bow to the chest, then back fisted him in the face as he injected the serum into his neck.

All of the wind stopped at once, and Juan looked around for Pharaoh and the Supreme mobile. Tapping the built-in transmitter to see where he was.

"Yo Bruh where you at?"

"I left and went to the East side" "Ok what's the next move again"

"While i'm on the Eastside,you have to go to Bankhead and handle that and we will meet back up downtown"

"Ok sounds like a plan, i'm leaving now" Supreme took off running leaving the

IceQueen and Cyclone laying there on the ground for the police to get.

13

While Pharaoh rode the streets of East Atlanta. He kept his head on a swivel, looking for an abnormal person running the streets. The police radar was picking up for a lot of bank robberies taking place. They say the person had the ability to make himself into a giant. As Pharaoh rode down Wesley Chapel, police were everywhere. He jumped on to Rainbow Dr and police were still flying up and down the street.

They were on the hunt for the suspect. Making a right on to Columbia Dr then a left onto McAfee rd. The Supreme mobile started to alert Pharaoh that something was going down at Glendale Park. As he turned into Glendale Park he slowly cruised the streets. Until he saw something that looked unreal. A guy was shrinking as he went over the small hill.

Pharaoh speeded the Supreme mobile up to meet the guy on the other side of the hill. Only to get over there and not see nothing. The man was nowhere in sight. Pharaoh flipped a switch and everything around him showed up on a grid. He could see the structure of everything. And with that he saw that the guy had a secret door on the hill.

Pharaoh saw a thermal heat motion moving inside the hill. His mind went to racing on how he was going to get him out of there and give him the cure. Pharaoh hit another switch and the passenger seat flipped down and opened up. He grabbed two flash bombs and got out of the car. Hitting a button on his watch to turn the Supreme mobile into stealth mode. Then switched his watch over to the grid so he could see the entrance. Pushing on the hill to open up the door.

As the ground shift and door opened, Pharaoh slowly walked inside. See the christmas lights hanging on the wall. Pharaoh knew he was str8 from the ghetto whoever he was. He multiplied himself so he could cover more ground.

One of the clones ran into a dead end, with only a few minutes of life time it disappeared. All of the other clones retracted themselves. All of the Intel that they collected downloaded into that one. And by this time Pharaoh had approached his target.

"Hey how did you get in here?" "I'm here to help you"

"I didn't ask for no help and who are you?"

"I'm the Doctor"

"What?! I didn't ask for no damn Doctor"

The guy took off towards Pharaoh. Running him up against the wall. Pharaoh tried to calm him down. But while he had him up against the wall, he realized that he was Dr.Johnson from D.N.A. That only made him madder. He started to slowly grow, Pharaoh kicked him on the inside of his leg. Taking his leg out as he uppercut him in the chin.

Making him release him, Pharaoh took off running. Grabbing the flash grenades off of his utility belt. Throwing them behind him as he headed for the door. The grenades went off and Stretch began to grow. Bursting through the ground, Pharaoh and money went flying everywhere.

Hitting up against a tree to brace his fall, Pharaoh shook it off and got up. With Stretch towering over the trees,Pharaoh knew it was going to be hard to get to him. As he hid behind the trees trying to come up with his plan. Stretch began to yell out his name.

"Doctor Johnson! come out come out wherever you are!" Stretch quickly scanned the area and spotted Pharaoh behind the trees. He headed his direction.

Pharaoh took off running from behind the trees. Coming out into the open to face him head up. Quickly cloning himself to throw Stretch off track. Making all of his clones run in different directions. Stretch didn't know who to go after. The sound of sirens got louder and louder.

DeKalb County Police were pulling up left and right. As they jumped out of their cars they released fire. The bullets were bouncing off him like rubber. Stretch took a swing at the police and knocked over a whole line of police cars. Sending the police on a frenzy.

Pharaoh used the distraction to make his move. Creeping up behind Stretch, he pulled out the sermon to stick him in the leg. But before he could inject him a police yelled for him to get out the way. And that alerted Stretch and got Pharaoh kicked across the field. Pharaoh hit the ground and rolled until he hit a news reporter's van. "Sir are you ok"

Getting up off his hands and knees he just looked at her and took off running. Stretch was on the move trying to get away from the police. Pharaoh hit a button on his watch and the Supreme mobile revealed itself. He quickly jumped in and took off behind him. And the police followed suit.

the disturbing thing to Pharaoh was how they were after him also. He heard over the transmitter that it was two suspects and not just one. Pharaoh shook his head and knew that he had to put an end to this. He speeded the Supreme mobile up.

Messing around with the screen inside of the car. He activated the bolas gun. Firing two bolases out at a time. The roped balls went flying around his feet and legs. Tripping him up and bringing him down. As Stretch went face first to the ground, Pharaoh speeded up. Quickly hitting a switch to change the gun mode.

He rode by and shot him with the serum and kept going. Looking in his rearview mirror to make sure it was working. Two police cars stayed on him while the rest stopped to apprehend Stretch. Once they put him inside of the police car, Pharaoh speeded up. The police speeded up as well and got on each side of him.

Coming over the loudspeaker telling him to pull over. Hiding behind the tinted windows, Pharaoh shot them a bird and went into overdrive. Spotting the little roadblock ahead, Pharaoh went off the grid and went into stealth cops slammed on breaks. Pharaoh went right through their little road block.

Calling Jaun up to see if he had everything under control.

"Yeah"

"Yo bruh bruh how are you coming along?" "Well I'm in the middle of something right now cant talk"

"Do you need my help?"

"No just head to downtown" "Ok I'm heading there now"

14

Coming in from Roswell everything looked okay. Until he jumped onto West Marietta st. It was light in some areas and dark in others. He kept on running until he got onto Joseph E. Lowery Blvd. That took him right into Bankhead,where it was pitch black.

Juan stopped and looked around. Thinking to himself that there was no way that could find the experiment. He didn't even know where to start. And besides that Bankhead wasn't a small area. The only thing he could think of was to go into supersonic speed and search the whole Bankhead.

Finally he caught a break through. Seeing a bright ball of light mixed with lightning bolts. Knowing that that could only mean one thing. Supreme took off in that direction. Slowing down to get a better look at what he was up against. All of the lights from Clark Atlanta shut off.

The experiment begins to shoot lightning out of his hands. Flipping over cars and hitting buildings creating fires. Juan ran up out of nowhere and struck him twice. Catching Power off guard only made him madder. He began to shoot lightning bolts at Supreme. Missing him only by inches.

As Supreme kept zigging and zagging around to dodge the lightning bolts, they were taking out everything that was behind him. Juan thought that this fight was going to be quick and easy. As he moved in on Power with his quick speed. But what he didn't know was Power had more tricks up his sleeve. As soon as Supreme went to swing at him, he was hit with a force field of lighten. The thin wall of lighten kept Juan from hitting him.

No matter how fast he runs around him to land a lick. The force field was there to stop him. Power sent a strong force of light out of the box. Grounding Supreme in his tracks for a hot second. The rubber on the bottom of his suit allowed the electricity to pass right through him. Supreme shook it off.

"Now that tickled"

"Who are you and what do you want with me?" "Well I'm Supreme and sad to say i'm here to stop you"

"Look I have no beef with you"

"Well that maybe true, but I can't let you destroy my city"

"Hell I'm from Center Hill but that doesn't matter now"

"Ok so what is it that you want?"

"I'm here to set an example, it's a new world order"

Standing there looking at the electricity run through his body. As he tried to figure out how he was going to stop him. People begin to come out of their dorm room. Crowding around and recording with their cell phones. It was too real to be true. The more the people came out the more Juan worried.

He knew that their curiosity was putting them in danger. Supreme begins to tell everyone to get back. In the midst of the crowd backing up people begin to be abducted. Supreme kept looking around for the screaming. But couldn't see where it was coming from, until he noticed everyone had their phones point at the sky. It was raining humans.

Placing his hands on his head as he looked at the giant bird flying off. He quickly snapped out of it and ran to catch everyone that was falling. As he sat them on the ground he spoke to himself."Not only do I have to deal with electric man, I got to fight a damn big ass bird too". He shook his head out of frustration and made his way back over to Power.

"Aye electric man! Let's gone and get this over with because if you ain't noticed I have a big ass bird to catch."

"My name is Power and that big fella is Owlite" "Man I don't give a fuck what you niggas name is, I just have to wrap this shit up"

"Your disrespectful and I'm going to teach you some manners"

Power quickly shot an electrical rope out of his hand. Wrapping it around Supreme and begin to pull him in closer to him. Supreme looked at him with a silly smirk, before he wrapped his hands around the rope. And doug his foot into the ground then snatch on the rope. Pulling Power forward before he shut off his electric energy.

Power looked at Supreme with a confused look as he slowly walked backwards. Trying his best to keep and eye on him before he turned around to run. As soon as he turned his back to Supreme, he was standing right in front of him. Power stumbles over his own feet trying to back up him. As he crawled backwards begging him to spare his life. Owlite came out of nowhere.

Swooping in grabbing Supreme by one of his legs and taking him for a ride. As Supreme dangled in mid air, he kept trying to grab a hold of Owlite's claw. Owlite had wings and claws like a bird but he also had human parts as well. As Supreme reached back up to try to grab Owlite again his build in transmitter went off. "Yeah"

"Yo bruh bruh how are you coming along?" "Well I'm in the middle of the of something right now cant talk"

"Do you need my help?"

"No just head to downtown" "Ok I'm heading there now"

Supreme let Pharaoh hang up as he swung his body forward.

Grabbing on to Owlite's clawed feet, he got just enough momentum to use his other leg to kick Owlite in the nuts. Owlite dropped him in mid air. Supreme flipped over from his back and placed his arms by his side. Swirling to the ground before he stuck out his arms.

Flipping in mid air before hitting the ground in his superhero landing polls. As he got off of his knee and stood up. He saw Power stealing energy from the light pole. He realized that he had to keep Power from powering up,so it would be easy to get around his little force field. Quickly running over to take out the lights pole and any other source of energy. Then switched over to night vision on his suit.

Seeing Power standing there growing was too much for the night vision. He quickly switched back over and attacked him. Going into a full body combat attack. Owlite flew right in and joined the fight. But they was no match for Supreme, when it came down to hand to hand combat.

Owlite flew off and left Power to fight. But within seconds he was swirling in. Attacking him as he flew by. That helped Power to deliver some strong and vital hits. Supreme shook them off as he backed up a little bit. Liking the way they were working together to go against him made him feel good. That only made him go harder.

As they began to go at it again, Owlite tried that same move. Supreme kicked Power in the chest and snatched Owlite out of the air by his foot slamming him to the ground. Seeing Power beginning to lose his glow, Supreme went to make his move. Owlite saw Supreme moving towards Power and he quickly thrusted his wings. Flying backwards by Supreme and scooped Power off the ground. Getting him close enough to the power line that was on the ground so he could charge up. As he pulled the little source of electricity off the line, Owlite turned his wings into a bronze shield.

He began to twirl around and the tip of his wings became blades. Cutting through the cars that were next to them. Supreme took two steps back then ran up his wings. As he opened up to throw Supreme off of him, Supreme quickly threw a syringe at him hitting him in the neck. As he landed Power was still struggling to get enough energy to fight with.

Supreme kicked him over and Power hit him some lightning to the chest. But it didn't even budge him. Supreme simply reached down and stuck him with the serum. Wasting no time he took off headed for downtown.

15

As Supreme ran through the streets of downtown Atlanta,he saw chow everywhere. Pulling up at D.N.A Agency everything seems so calm in the area. Supreme turned on the transmitter and called Pharaoh.

"Hello"

"Where you at?"

"I'm parked across the street,I was about to call you when the sensor off"

"What sensor and what's the plan for the attack here?"

"Nevermind how I knew you was here, I'm on my way over"

Supreme looked around to see the whereabouts of Pharaoh. He spotted him getting out the Supreme mobile, but to the necked eye it would look like he appeared out of thin air.

"So what's the plan here smart guy"

"Well before I came down here I went back to the cabin. I made some smoke and flash bombs that releases the cure into the air. All they have to do is inhale it."

"Damn you should have been came up with this shit all that damn fighting you made me do"

"Better late than never. Look I'm going to put the smoke bombs in the ventilation system so it can spread. And you take the flash bombs with you,use as needed"

"Hold on! Will this shit cure me as well?" "No it's all made from our D.N.A"

"Oh shit they still my D.N.A on file, so it might dont work if they are made from my blood" "That's true but we have to try"

"Aye when your done at the ventilation system go to the lab and destroy all records with my D.N.A on it"

"Ok I got you little bro but before you go in give me 10 minutes"

"No problem just hurry up"

Pharaoh hit a button on his suit and went into stealth mode. Supreme continued cutting through the parking lot. The closer he got the better the guards realized who he was. They began walking towards him,while hitting the radio to let Mr.Beans know he was there. Supreme ran up and took them out and kept going.

As he entered the agency it was like a ghost town. Supreme took off running through the hallway. There were bodies laid out everywhere. He knew that Pharaoh had made it to the ventilation system. The alarm went off and the lights turned red. Supreme knew it was go time from that point on.

"Yo Supreme" "Yeah bro I'm here"

"Ok im headed to the lab area now, keep your eyes open"

"Oh yeah I already know"

While they both were on different missions, Mr.Beans came over the intercom. "Welcome back Mr.Johnson, I knew you would come back". Supreme knew exactly where Mr.Beans was. While Mr.Beans was talking over the intercom he was calling in all of his experiments. Looking at his big monitor screen to see who was still alive. He knew it was going to take everything he had.

Seeing that all of his experiments were heading back to the agency,he took off through a secret passageway. A minute too late Supreme came bursting through the door. Looking around the room for Mr.Beans, knowing that he had to be there. Pounding his fist on the edge of the desk out of frustration and anger. He remembered when he was head enforcer, Mr.Beans would go into a secret room. Supreme quickly ran over to the area he remembered seeing him go to.

Feeling on the wall for the switch that opened the door. Hearing the clicking sound from the door opening, Supreme stopped and pushed on the door. As the door opened he saw the monitor screens and controls. Walking all the way in to get a better look at things. He forgot all about Mr.Beans not being in there. He was shocked by how many people that Mr.Beans had done changed over.

There were so many red dots on the screen headed in his direction, he couldn't even think about Mr.Beans.

"Yo Pharaoh"

"Yeah bro I'm here what's up?"

"Man they coming in hot and it's a lot of them" "What are you talking about Supreme?" "Everyone that he changed is coming back to the agency"

"Oh shit that's a lot of heat! I'm still in the lab,

let me see what I can come up with to help out" "Ok well make it quick because they are coming"

Supreme looked at the control panel to see if it was a way to stop them. But he couldn't figure it out. He began to hit any button that he thought would do it. Mr.Beans popped up on the screen.

"I see you made it to my secret control room. But I have what you're looking for"

Mr.Beans held up a remote then smiled as he vanished off the screen. Supreme yelled and slammed his fist on the control panel breaking it in half. Leaving back out of the control room more frustrated than before. Not knowing that he was inches away from

Mr.Bean's escape chamber. As he made his way back through the hallway, he noticed that they were clear.

The bodies that were there before weren't anymore. And before he knew it, he went flying through the air. As he hit the wall to brace his fall, he tried to figure out what tripped him. Only to see one of Mr.Beans soldiers revealing themselves. Supreme got up and cracked his knuckles.

Engaging into combat with the soldier. They would go back and forth delivering hits. But Supreme couldn't get a whole of him like he wanted. Everytime he thought he had him he would disappear. That made Supreme frustrated because he just fought Cyclone, and he did the same thing.

Trying to see if he had a pattern, so he could grab him. But as he stood there waiting for him to attack again, he realized that he was gone. Blackman revealed himself at the end of the hallway. Supreme took off after him, knowing deep down inside it was a trap. Everytime he got close or headed Blackman way he would disappear. Only revealing himself long enough for Supreme to see him.

Leading him back to the front lobby. Where it was a gang of soldiers waiting on him. Mr.Beans was standing on the first level looking over the balcony. Supreme noticed that Mr.Beans had Gabby and a few other soldiers with him. He looked at Gabby, but she showed no signs of sorrow.

Supreme knew that it was all business from that point on. He took off running into the crowd. Slowing everything down made it more easy for him to wipe them out. But as he took them out more came. Even at supersonic speed he couldn't handle all of the soldiers that were coming in. He fought one or two of them at a time and ran to the next soldier.

Mr.Beans stood on the upper level watching. As Supreme started to get a handle on things more experiments came. But this batch was stronger than the first. Supreme continued to fight but was overpowered by them. They piled on top of Supreme trying to tear him apart. Supreme tried his best not to give in.

All he heard was Pharaoh's voice in the back of his head, telling him not to give up. Supreme stops moving and begins to pull in energy. With his mind clear,his thoughts were a lot better. As his energy began to get stronger he began to glow. His energy light began to show through the cracks of everyone that was piled on him. Supreme reached down and pulled the small flash bombs off his belt.

Releasing the bombs at the same time he activated his energy bomb. Soldiers went flying in every direction. Supreme was standing in the middle of the lobby glowing. He looked up and pointed at Mr.Beans. His eyes got big and he took a step back while tapping Gabby and the other soldiers on the shoulders.

Signifying them to attack. They all jumped over the balcony. And before they hit the ground, Supreme took off in attack mode. Not even giving them a chance to make the first move. Every chance one of the soldiers got they would use their powers.

Earthman would shake or move the ground to try to mess up Supreme steps. But Supreme was always a step ahead. He made sure he took out Blankman first. Because he knew it's hard to take out something you can't see. And as soon as he thought about it, he hadn't seen Gabby in a minute.

Seconds later she made herself bigger and was on Supreme's back. Trying to put him in a choke hold. Supreme quickly speeded up, then stopped very hard,sending Gabby flying off his back. With no time to spare he had to dodge shots from Beam. He was shooting lasers out of his eye. As Supreme went into supersonic speed, Pharaoh came over the transmitter.

"I got it bro"

"Well it's about time because I need you"

"Ok I need you to bring them closer to me and I will shoot them with this new cure gun" "Hold up where the hell are you?"

"I'm up here, but don't look. We have to catch them off guard"

"Ok and I see you too,I'm headed your way" As Supreme led them closer to Pharaoh,

while he got his aim ready. Not seeing Crawler creeping down the wall behind him. "Pharaoh watch out behind you" Supreme yelled. Pharaoh quickly duplicated himself and shot Crawler with the gun. The bullet that came out the gun turned into a net. And wrapped

Crawler up, while it shocked the cure into him.

Supreme saw that and speeded up. Running circles around them then using his super strength I told them in the air one at a time. Pharaoh shot them as they came flying in the air.

16

Meanwhile Mr.Beans was slowly trying to escape, while Supreme was occupied. As soon as Supreme finished circling then,he counted to make sure everyone was accounted for. The cure net was doing its job just like Pharaoh planned. The micro fibers from the net were poking into their skin. Sending out shocks that released the cure inside of them.

Supreme looked around and didn't see Mr.Beans anywhere.

"Yo Pharaoh where he go?"

"Don't worry about it,he can't get far" "What do you mean?"

"Oh I have the place on lockdown and am at every door"

Hearing a door close behind them they both turned around. Mr.Beans was walking towards them holding Gabby hostage. Supreme was looking confused because he thought Gabby was in one of the nets. Mr.Beans told Supreme not to move or he would activate the chip to go off inside of her. And Supreme looked over at Pharaoh and Pharaoh signaled for him to hold on.

"So what is it that you want now?"Pharaoh asked

"You know what I want, World Genocide to put my people back on top."

"See now that's that bullshit, it doesn't matter what goes on in this world today racism will always play a part" Supreme yelled out right before he took off. Running in supersonic speed he was able to grab the remote right out of his hand. Snapping the remote into two.

Sent Gabby into kill mode. She grabbed Mr.Beans by the rist and flipped him over her shoulders.

Then quickly snapped his neck and went after Supreme. Supreme deflected each attack she made. "Gabby what are you doing? It's over now let us help you" Supreme stated while he stayed in defense mode. Gabby didn't say a word she just kept attacking. Supreme grabbed her and wrapped his arms around her. "Gabby its me Supreme I'm here to help"

"Can't be helped it's too late"

"No your wrong look around you, didn't no one die today but the ones that really needed too. Let Pharaoh help you"

Gabby continued to squirm around in Supreme's arms before trying to kick him in the head. Supreme quickly released her with a little push. Standing back looking at her as she cracked her knuckles. Supreme shook his head,with a look on his face as if he didn't want to do it. He threw his hands and waited for her to make her move.

Gabby took off running towards Supreme. And Pharaoh shot at her with his net gun. Before she could even shrink the net was on her and working.

"Sorry I left you bro but I had to make some adjustments to the gun."

"Well damn you could have let me know I thought you left me hanging"

"Come on lil bro you know I would never do that. And sorry about your little girlfriend" "Its ok she was crazy anyways"

As they headed to the exit door Supreme looked over at Pharaoh and smiled. Then asked him if he destroyed all of the files. Pharaoh just smiled back and nodded his head, while he placed his arm around Supreme neck. As soon as they stepped outside,the police had them surrounded.

"Freeze"

"Man we the good guys" Pharaoh shouted out with his hands in the air. Supreme looked at him and told him that they didn't care about all that. We two niggas in a suit. We need to get out of here fast. Pharaoh dropped his hands and disappeared. Supreme took off running at supersonic speed. The cops were lost; they didn't know what just happened or where they went.

Printed in the United States
by Baker & Taylor Publisher Services